KAPTIVA
THE SHRIEKING SIREN

BY ADAM BLADE

ORCHARD

With special thanks to Tabitha Jones

www.beastquest.co.uk

ORCHARD BOOKS

First published in Great Britain in 2022 by Hodder & Stoughton

3 5 7 9 10 8 6 4 2

Text © Beast Quest Limited 2022
Cover and inside illustrations by Steve Sims and Dynamo Ltd
© Beast Quest Limited 2022

Beast Quest is a registered trademark of Beast Quest Limited
Series created by Beast Quest Limited, London

A CIP catalogue record for this book is available from the British Library.

ISBN 978 1 40836 540 3

Printed in Great Britain

The paper and board used in this book are made from wood from responsible sources

Orchard Books
An imprint of Hachette Children's Group
Part of Hodder & Stoughton
Carmelite House, 50 Victoria Embankment, London EC4Y 0DZ

An Hachette UK Company
www.hachette.co.uk
www.hachettechildrens.co.uk

Welcome to the world of Beast Quest!

Tom was once an ordinary village boy, until he travelled to the City, met King Hugo and discovered his destiny. Now he is the Master of the Beasts, sworn to defend Avantia and its people against Evil. Tom draws on the might of the magical Golden Armour, and is protected by powerful tokens granted to him by the Good Beasts of Avantia. Together with his loyal companion Elenna, Tom is always ready to visit new lands and tackle the enemies of the realm.

While there's blood in his veins, Tom will never give up the Quest…

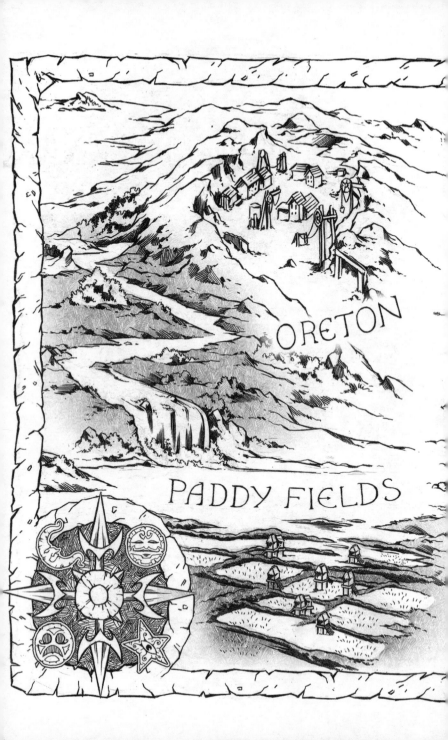

TANGALA

PANIA

ARAN

There are special gold coins to collect in this book. You will earn one coin for every chapter you read.

Find out what to do with your coins at the end of the book.

CONTENTS

You thought I was gone, did you not? Swallowed by the Netherworld, never to set foot in the upper world again... Consumed by the Beasts that roam this foul place... Well, it's not that easy to be rid of the most powerful magician who ever stalked the land.

I have the perfect plan up my sleeve, and soon I shall leave this Realm of Beasts behind.

And the best part? My arch enemy Tom will die in the process.

See you all very soon!

Malvel

AN ILL WIND

"Wait!" Elenna said, her voice so hoarse Tom could barely hear it over the howl of the wind. He turned, glad to put his back to the constant icy blast that knifed through his clothes and hurled grit into his eyes. They had been trudging over seemingly endless mounds of black volcanic rock beneath the dreary

purple sky of the Netherworld.
Under a layer of grime, Elenna's
face was grey with exhaustion
and covered in scratches and cuts.
She took a swig from her flask,
grimacing at the taste. Tom's own
throat was parched, but the water
they had taken from Styx's foul-
smelling swamp only seemed to
make him thirstier.

Tom and Elenna were on a Quest
to rescue four young warriors
from the clutches of Tom's
oldest enemy, the Dark Wizard,
Malvel. The children had been
competing to become the new
Master or Mistress of the Beasts
for the kingdom of Tangala. Malvel

had kidnapped them during the contest, transporting them to the Beast-infested wastelands of the Netherworld. The villain was now demanding that Tom give his magical purple jewel in exchange for the contestants' lives. If Malvel got his hands on it, he'd be able to use the jewel to open a portal and escape this prison world. Tom couldn't allow that to happen.

Since crossing through Daltec's portal in search of the young heroes, Tom and Elenna had defeated two Beasts – the giant jackal, Ossiron, and the swamp monster, Styx – and sent Nolan and Katya back to Tangala using the purple jewel Malvel craved. But two more candidates, Miandra and Rafe, were still lost somewhere in the Netherworld, at the mercy of Beasts under the control of the evil sorcerer.

"Surely we have to be close to the next Beast now?" Elenna said.

"I'll check," Tom said, pulling the map of the Netherworld that Daltec had given him from his tunic.

"Still not dead, then?" a familiar, cheerful voice piped up from the parchment. It belonged to Zarlo, the ancient Avantian wizard who had created the map, only to become somehow locked inside it.

Ignoring the wizard, Tom scanned the map, quickly locating a small purple dot that pulsed faintly near a hastily sketched outline of a forest.

"You're only halfway through your Quest, you know?" Zarlo went on. "And already you smell *terrible...*" The formless wizard coughed theatrically. "In fact, do you mind holding my map a bit further away?"

Elenna gave an exasperated growl. "What do you expect? We just fought a swamp monster," she said. "And how can you smell us, anyway? You don't even have a nose!"

"How rude!" the wizard snapped indignantly. "I'll have you know that I—"

"Hush!" Tom hissed, holding

the map close to his face so Zarlo would hear him. The wind had risen suddenly to a wild, piercing shriek. Turning to frown at the horizon, Tom spotted a dense wall of black dust tearing towards them at impossible speed. "Elenna, look out!" he cried, just as a gust slammed into him, shoving him backwards and almost snatching the map from his hands. Elenna staggered as the wind swirled around them, forcing dust into their lungs, making them both cough and choke.

Narrowing his eyes, Tom saw the dust cloud come together before them, swirling to become a vast, towering shape he knew only too well: a tall, hooded figure with cavernous cheeks and a cruel, skeletal grin. *Malvel!* The wizard let out a triumphant  howl of laughter as Tom and Elenna bent low against the buffeting wind, fighting to keep their footing.

"That's right...*cower* before me!" Malvel boomed. "You cannot begin to imagine the power I wield! I will make you one final offer. Hand over your purple jewel, and I will return the worthless children you seek unharmed. Withhold it from me, and they shall perish in agony, far away from home!"

Tom thought of Miandra and Rafe, remembering how proudly they had stood before Prince Rotu at the start of the trials, only days before. They were both so young and filled with promise, and now they were trapped in a barren land populated by Beasts... *I can't let them die here*, Tom thought, his hand creeping towards the purple jewel in his belt. *With the candidates safe, I could fight Malvel without risking their lives. Then I would be free to put all my focus on defeating him once and for all!*

Elenna gripped Tom's shoulder. "You can't trust Malvel," she hissed in his ear. "Do as he says, and Rafe and Miandra will be trapped here for ever."

Tom let his hand fall away from the jewel. Elenna was right. The Dark Wizard had never once kept his word in their many previous battles. Tom drew himself up against the force of the wind to stand tall. "Forget it, Malvel!" he shouted back. "We came here to defeat you, and that's what we'll do. Just as we have done every other time we've fought!"

Malvel's hideous grin vanished. His

hollow eyes narrowed with hatred. "Then they shall die here in the Netherworld!" he cried. "And so shall you. I am more than happy to wait while you starve in this wilderness. I'll be more than happy to prise the jewel from the rotting remains of your corpse." With a deafening howl of wind, the wizard's shadowy form dissolved into eddying tendrils of dust. The buffeting gale died away, leaving behind a sudden calm. Tom breathed a sigh of relief...

But then a single violent gust tore Zarlo's map from his hand.

"No!" Tom cried as the parchment was whisked away, up into the purple sky.

"Help!" Zarlo wailed.

Tom raced after the map, about to call on the magical jumping ability of his golden boots – part of an  enchanted suit of armour stored safely in Avantia, with powers he could access from anywhere. But then he stopped. There was no point in leaping. The parchment was already far out of reach. Zarlo's panicked cries dwindled as the map spun higher and quickly vanished from sight.

THE POISONED FOREST

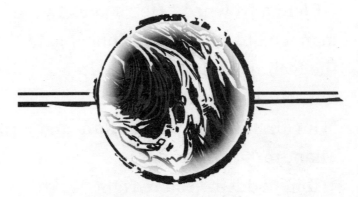

"How will we find our way around this horrible place now?" Elenna asked.

Tom let out a weary sigh. "I can use the magic of my yellow jewel to remember the map," he said. "I'm pretty sure I can get us close to where Zarlo marked the nearest

Beast. But I feel bad. Zarlo might be annoying, but we can't just abandon him."

Elenna frowned. "He's somehow managed to survive this long. I get the feeling Zarlo can look after himself for a while," she said. "Our first duty is to find Rafe and Miandra."

Tom nodded. "You're right. We'd better get moving – we still have a way to go."

After that, they walked in silence, shoulders bent into the wind as their boots crunched over the shifting mounds of gravel. Tom's legs ached more with each step and his head swam with hunger and thirst.

Elenna's teeth were chattering, and Tom's fingers and toes were so cold he could hardly feel them. Still, he reminded himself that Rafe and Miandra were probably just as cold and hungry as they were. Maybe more. And the two young candidates had no idea that help was coming. Tom forced himself to move faster, willing them not to lose hope.

With the heavy sky the same dark, bruised shade of purple in every direction, it was hard to tell how much time passed as they walked. Tom felt as if they had travelled for half a day at least – but finally, he spotted a line of spindly, skeletal trees on the horizon.

"That must be the forest on the map," he said. "Or what remains of it." From a distance, it looked as if a fire had raged through the trees, burning away the leaves until nothing but charred trunks remained.

As they drew closer, Tom caught a musty whiff of rotting wood instead of the smoke he would have expected, and he saw the trees were diseased rather than scorched. Bark hung in tattered strips from their blackened trunks, and the crumbling remnants of fallen branches littered the ground. The cold wind whipped up eddies of leaf litter that spun

in the air like black snow. As Tom
stepped into the shadowy forest,
layers of dry bark and twigs cracked
underfoot. The acrid stench of
mould rose
sharply,
making him
catch his
breath.

"I've never
seen a forest
so dead,"
Elenna said,
shivering.
"It's exactly
the sort of
place you'd
expect to find a Beast."

Tom nodded. "But at least we should see it coming. There's nowhere to hide."

Stepping over twisted branches, they picked their way between the tortured-looking trees. Rotten holes gaped in trunks like wailing mouths and the wind moaned, swirling in fitful gusts that churned up more flakes of dead wood. The stench of death and decay was almost overpowering. Tom covered his mouth and nose with his sleeve, but he could still taste the bitter mould in the air. He felt the rasping tingle of dust and spores reaching deep into his lungs. The dark specks whirling around him made him feel queasy, like he was on a rocking boat out on a choppy sea. He shook his head to clear the dizziness, but that only made his stomach churn more. At his side, Elenna stumbled. Tom put out a hand to steady her, and he saw her lips were almost white and her short hair was damp with sweat.

"Can you go on?" he asked in alarm.

"That swamp water..." Elenna said weakly. "I think...it's making me sick."

Tom realised now he was sweating too – his skin felt clammy despite the cold. He swallowed hard, trying to settle his stomach. "Me too," he said. But then he noticed something strange. The ground beneath his boots seemed to be moving...rising and falling ever so slightly. *It can't be!* he thought. But his eyes were seeing it swell and deflate, almost like the forest was...

Breathing?

Tom shuddered and dropped to his knees, pushing his palms down into the leaf litter. He could feel a slow, rolling movement, like the swell of the sea. *No wonder we feel sick!*

"What is it?" Elenna asked.

"The ground..." Tom hissed, gesturing for her to join him. Elenna knelt at his side.

Her eyes widened as she too

put her palms to the earth. "Oh, no," she groaned. "This has to be a nightmare."

"The forest isn't dead at all," Tom said. "This whole place is alive!" He shot to his feet and hastily rubbed the clinging dirt from his hands.

Elenna rose too, her eyes round with horror. "What do we do?" she asked.

"We keep going," Tom said. "We find Miandra and Rafe. Then we get away from this place, as fast as we can."

Now that Tom knew what was making him nauseous, he did his best to adjust his gait to roll with the sickening rise and fall of the ground while he kept his eyes fixed on the horizon. But even as his nausea receded, the wind grew steadily stronger, filling the air with rot until he could barely see three paces ahead. Vile black flakes swarmed around his face like flies as he and Elenna forged silently onward through a world of tumbling greys.

"Tom, look!" Elenna cried suddenly, pointing at a nearby trunk. Narrowing his eyes, Tom saw splotches of sickly yellow-brown gloop clinging to the bark. He peered closer and gasped. The liquid had hardened to a glassy resin, and he could make out horrible, twisted shapes trapped within.

There were clumps of mangy feathers all pasted together, and taloned feet curled stiffly in death. "Janus birds!" Tom said. He counted three of them. The creatures' eyes

were open and their beaks gaped, frozen for ever in a final gasp.

Elenna frowned sadly. "What a terrible way to die…

How could it have happened?"

Tom shook his head as he ran his gaze over the tangled mess. "I don't know," he said. "Nothing makes any sense in this hideous place."

"Tom!" Elenna gasped, grabbing his arm and pointing to a crusted puddle of amber on the ground. Another dark shape had been locked inside its murky prison – but this shape wasn't a bird's. It was a metal trident with a gemstone set into the hilt. Cold, sick dread washed over Tom. He had last seen that weapon clasped in the hand of a brave young warrior.

"It's Miandra's," Tom said, his eyes flicking involuntarily back to the

entombed Janus birds. *Please don't
let us be too late!*

A DEADLY PRISON

As Tom and Elenna gazed down at Miandra's fallen weapon – now a relic encased in amber – the wind shrieked around them like evil laughter.

Tom drew his sword and began to hack at the amber, chipping it away. "Help me," he said. "When we find

Miandra, she'll want this back. And if we don't find her..." Tom trailed off, unwilling to voice the thought that the girl's family would want something to remember her by.

"We'll find her," Elenna said firmly. Then she pulled an arrow from her quiver and knelt, using its tip to chisel away the resin. It was as hard and brittle as flint, and Tom's muscles soon burned from the effort, but far worse was the guilty dread that chilled his heart.

"If I hadn't insisted we hold trials in Tangala, Miandra would never have come to Pania," Tom muttered. "She would never have been abducted."

"You can't think like that," Elenna said, prising another chunk of amber free. "Tangala is under constant threat from Beasts. It badly needs a champion. Without one, everyone there is at risk – not just Miandra. Holding the trials was the right thing to do."

Tom knew Elenna spoke sense, but he still couldn't shake the feeling that he'd made a terrible mistake that would cost innocent lives. He tried to put this thought from his mind and focus instead on the job at hand.

Finally, between them, Tom and Elenna removed the last chips of amber from around the trident.

 As he pulled the weapon free, Tom heard a high, distant shout. He and Elenna both froze, listening.

"Help!" the voice called again. It was a girl, somewhere in the distance.

"Miandra!" Elenna said. "She's alive." With the trident in one hand and his sword in the other, Tom ran towards the sound.

"Wait! Where are you going?" Elenna called after him.

Stopping, Tom turned back, puzzled. "To find her!"

"But she's over that way," Elenna said, pointing in the opposite direction.

"Help!" Miandra called again – her voice definitely coming from the way that Tom had been headed.

"No," he said, gesturing impatiently. "She's over *there*!"

Elenna frowned. "It doesn't sound like that to me. Could an echo be distorting the sound?"

Tom thought for a moment. Elenna seemed so sure. "It's possible," he said. "Everything here is strange.

We'd better split up and hope one of us is right."

Elenna nodded. "But whether we find her or not, we both need to meet back here before dark."

"Good plan," Tom said. "Let's mark the trees so we can find our way back – keep your eyes peeled for any sign of the Beast."

At that moment, Miandra shouted again, and Tom and Elenna both sprinted away, heading in different directions.

Tom hurried through the trees, keeping as close to a straight line as he could, bounding over the unsteady ground. Every few steps, he slashed the trunk of a tree at head height, scoring the bark with his sword. Though the wind masked most sounds, he could hear Miandra's calls getting louder as he went.

"Miandra!" Tom called back – but when he heard her shout again, she sounded like she hadn't heard him. The ashy blizzard thickened, the flakes becoming larger until he was constantly batting them away. He pulled his tunic up over his mouth and nose to keep the debris out of his lungs, but it was hard to get enough air. Still, he kept his thoughts fixed on Miandra, all alone and possibly hurt. Her calls were oddly muffled but seemed very near.

She has to be close!

"Miandra!" Tom called again.

"Hello?" she answered – and now Tom could hear an urgent, hopeful note in her voice.

"It's Tom," he called back. "Keep shouting so I can find you."

"I'm over here!" the girl cried, more urgently than ever. Tom could now hear banging and hammering too. He soon arrived at an open clearing. In the centre, just visible through the whirling blackness, stood the broad, knobbly stump of an ancient tree. A wide fissure in the trunk was crusted over with orangey-brown resin. The hammering was coming from inside. Tom could see something moving in the darkness of the tree's heart... *Miandra's stuck in that tree!*

As Tom hurried over, Miandra pressed her hands and face to the amber that imprisoned her.

"Please get me out," she said. "I'm running out of air!"

"Crouch down," Tom told her. She quickly did as he had asked. Tom ran his eyes over the amber, looking for any chinks or cracks – but it was as smooth as glass. Calling on the enhanced strength of his golden breastplate, he drew back his arm.

BOOF! Tom slammed his fist into the amber, splintering it and smashing a hole. Miandra gasped, sucking in a huge breath.

"Thank you!" she said. Tom started to rip away the broken shards of amber, while Miandra pushed from inside. Before long, the opening

was large enough for her to squeeze through.

As she stepped from the trunk, Tom saw Miandra had a swollen, dark bruise the size of an egg on her forehead, and her fingernails were bloody and torn. *She must have been trying to claw her way free!*

Before Tom could even ask if she was all right, the girl dropped into a low bow. "You saved my life," she said, fixing him with solemn brown eyes. "While there is breath in my body, I swear, I shall repay you." Suddenly Miandra frowned, peering past Tom into the churning greyness. "But where is my mother?" she asked.

"Your mother?" Tom echoed. "She's back in Tangala. You were transported here through a magic portal."

The girl shook her head. "I must respectfully disagree. I know my mother's voice. I heard her calling to me as I tried to find my way out of this wood. She was close by, and as I ran to reach her, I must have hit my head on a branch." Miandra touched the huge bruise on her head. "I was knocked unconscious, and when I awoke, I was trapped as you found me."

Tom frowned. "I *saw* you and three other candidates pass through the portal. No one else. This forest is devious, though – it plays tricks on the mind."

Miandra's face was uncertain, but she bowed again. "I must hope it is as you say," she answered. "If my mother were here and still living, she would never have left me in that trunk." Her eyes blazed suddenly bright. "But if you are wrong, and someone has harmed her, I swear they will pay."

Tom couldn't help being impressed by the young girl's courage and determination. But as he glanced at the tree behind her, another, more unsettling thought stirred in his breast. Someone – or *something* – had put Miandra in that trunk and trapped her there.

And whoever it was, they never meant for her to get out alive.

4

KAPTIVA'S PROMISE

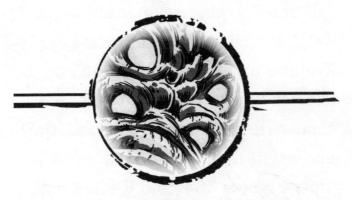

"Follow me," Tom said, handing
Miandra her trident. "We need to
find Elenna." He turned back the
way he had come, searching for the
marks he had left on the trees as he
traced his path through the gloomy
shadows, looking for the spot
where he and Elenna had agreed to
meet. Though the sky above was still

the dull purple of the Netherworld day, beneath the trees, the constant fall of ashy bark made it almost dark. Miandra walked briskly, easily keeping up with Tom despite her shorter stride and head injury. Far sooner than Tom had expected, they arrived at the patch of shattered amber where Tom and Elenna had found Miandra's trident – but there was no sign of Elenna. Tom was about to suggest they sit and wait, when he suddenly heard a panicked cry from behind them.

"Tom! Where are you?" Elenna's voice was shrill and urgent.

Tom turned sharply, breaking into a run. "Quick!" he told Miandra.

"Elenna's in trouble." They raced through the gloom, leaping over roots, lurching and staggering as the forest floor roiled beneath them.

"Tom!" Elenna cried again. Tom's heart clenched with fear at the terror in her voice. He pushed himself to run faster than ever, gasping for breath, cold sweat drenching his skin.

"You found her!" Elenna said, her voice coming from right behind him this time. Tom skidded to a stop, spinning around and almost colliding with Miandra. Beyond the young candidate, Elenna was emerging from between two trees, grinning with relief.

Miandra gasped. "I don't understand," she said. "How can you be here?"

Elenna frowned, suddenly noticing their puzzled faces.

"We thought you were in trouble," Tom told her. "We heard you calling from back that way." He gestured through the trees.

"I *was* calling," Elenna said,

"but not from over there. And I'm fine. Look." She held up Miandra's jewelled fishing net. "I found this hanging from a tree."

"This place is impossible!" Tom growled. "The trees must be doing something to our voices. But how?"

Elenna shrugged. "I don't know. But since we've found Miandra, we can get out of here. Hopefully we'll never even see the Beast that Malvel set to guard her."

Tom nodded. Normally, he would insist they find the Beast to break Malvel's hold over it. But he was beginning to wonder if the forest itself might be their true enemy – and if that was the case, it was an enemy they could never hope to defeat.

"You're right," he said, reaching for the yellow jewel in his belt and bringing his memory of Zarlo's map into his mind. Glancing around, he saw they were in a small, triangular clearing. He recognised it from the map – it was deep in the forest, nearest to the eastern border. "We have to go this way," he told Elenna and Miandra, striking off towards the way out.

The light was failing quickly now, and the wind had changed direction, driving flakes of mouldy bark directly into Tom's face. Each gust grew stronger and stronger until Tom was having to fight for every step. The movement of the ground had intensified too. It pitched and rolled under Tom's feet like the deck of a ship during  a storm. Glancing back at Miandra and Elenna, he saw they had linked arms to keep from falling, their faces set grimly as they struggled on.

"I almost feel as if the forest knows we're trying to escape..." Elenna gasped. "Like it doesn't want us to leave."

"It is more than that," Miandra said. "It wants us dead. I *would* be dead if Tom hadn't found me."

"You're right," Tom said. "Let's hurry!" They all picked up their pace, despite the driving wind and lurching ground.

Suddenly, a sharp jolt like a lightning strike fizzed through Tom's body. The shock was so strong that he froze, a burning heat spreading to the top of his head and the tips of his fingers and toes. It was coming from the red jewel in his belt. He touched the gem and felt a wave of fury slam into him, so intense it took his breath away. A hideous, creaking voice like dry branches snapping in the wind echoed through his mind: *You three fools will never escape Kaptiva's forest!*

"Are you hurt?" Elenna asked as she and Miandra stopped at his side.

Tom shook his head, slowly coming back to his own senses. "No, I'm fine," he said. "But I can hear the Beast's voice. She's called Kaptiva. She's close by – and she knows we're here. We need to..." Tom trailed off, his gaze alighting on a crooked tree a little way beyond Miandra. It was twisted with rot, just like all the others, with a sparse spread of bare, decaying branches – but he felt

almost sure it hadn't been there a moment before. He pointed. "This is going to sound odd, but has that tree moved?"

As Miandra and Elenna turned towards the tree, four glowing slits appeared in its broad trunk, quickly widening to become blazing orbs. Tom gasped. *The tree has eyes!*

And they were staring directly at him, burning with such intense rage, he felt as if they were boring right into his soul.

THE TREE-BEAST ATTACKS

Brandishing his sword, Tom ran his eyes up and down Kaptiva's gnarled trunk, looking for any sign of a weak spot. His blade was not made to fell trees. *If only we had Katya and her axe!* Beneath the Beast's two blazing eyes, another red gash opened, widening to become a gaping mouth

lined with sharp splinters of wood.
Glowing orange amber dripped from
between the Beast's jagged teeth
like drool, hardening and darkening
as it pooled on the ground. Kaptiva
emitted a harsh cracking sound like
hundreds of branches all snapping
at once, and Tom realised that she
was laughing.

*Your puny weapon cannot harm
me, human*, she cried, speaking
directly into Tom's mind. The Beast's
cavernous maw yawned wider,
revealing oozing amber bubbling
inside. Her red eyes flared like coals
at the heart of a forge.

"We fight together," Miandra said,
stepping to Tom's left, her trident

ready in her hand and her narrow
shoulders squared. At Tom's right,
Elenna fitted an arrow to her bow
and took aim. Kaptiva laughed

again – a wet, bubbling wheeze this time. Elenna fired an arrow straight into the tree-Beast's open mouth, but instead of hitting rotten wood, the missile sank out of sight. Still laughing, Kaptiva swivelled her red eyes downwards, fixing them on Miandra. Suddenly, Kaptiva vomited, ejecting a gush of glowing resin. Tom hooked his arm around Miandra and lifted her clear just before the vile jet struck the girl square in the chest. As Tom heard the heavy splat of liquid amber hitting a tree behind them, he thought of the dead Janus birds – and how close Miandra had been to sharing their horrible fate.

"Go!" Tom hissed to Miandra, setting her back on her feet. Kaptiva was already opening her giant mouth again, more resin pooling within its vast depths. Tom charged towards the Beast, drawing back his sword like an axe.

One of Kaptiva's crooked branches whipped out to slap the weapon from his grasp with such force his whole arm went limp. Half blinded with pain, he registered another, thicker branch swiping towards his face. Tom ducked sideways, but a sharp, low bough stabbed him in the gut, driving the air from his body, doubling him over with pain. Weak with nausea, he struggled for breath.

Choking bile burned his throat. *I'm being beaten up by a tree!* As Tom coughed and retched, he heard a *twang* followed by a *thud!* This time, Elenna's arrow had sunk deep into Kaptiva's trunk.

The Beast a let out a hideous, bubbling screech, sending globs of amber flying from her mouth like spittle. Her branches writhed in agony and her red eyes bulged. *Good shot, Elenna!* With a series of mighty pops and cracks, snaking white roots rose from the earth all around Kaptiva like a seething mass of giant worms. The forest floor rocked and heaved, almost throwing Tom over. With another

screech, Kaptiva turned and began
to glide away, walking on her
knotted mass of pale roots. Elenna
sent another arrow slamming into
the Beast's retreating trunk. Kaptiva
screeched again.

Spotting his weapon nearby, Tom
lunged towards it, but before he
could grip the hilt, something
snatched hold of his ankle and
tugged. He hit the ground hard,
turning to see that a thick white root
was coiled tight about his leg. His
stomach lurched as Kaptiva yanked
him over the forest floor, dragging
him along behind her.

"Tom!" Elenna cried, her voice
already sounding a long way off. His

body hit a tree which scraped his
side, ripping his clothes and tearing
at his flesh. He smashed into another
rotting trunk, then another. It was
like being pulled by a runaway
carthorse.

His whole body screamed with
pain as he crashed through the

forest, but Tom forced himself to think. *I have to get free before I'm skinned alive!* With no sword to save himself, he called on the magical strength from his golden breastplate, gripped his shield in both hands and bent double; then, still bumping and jolting over the rough earth, he chopped at the root with the edge of his shield. For a moment, it looked as if the blow had made no impact – but then the root began to splinter. Tom chopped again, severing the last woody fibres, and tumbled free, eventually rolling to a stop. Gasping and wincing, he heaved himself to his feet. Kaptiva was slithering away from him, fleeing through the forest on her raft of sinuous roots.

Elenna and Miandra hurried
to Tom's side.

"Here," Miandra said, handing Tom
his sword. "You will need this to win
this fight."

Tom took his weapon gratefully,
impressed once more by the young
warrior's steely resolve. Miandra's
slender frame only came up to Tom's
shoulder, but her eyes blazed with
a courage that would put many
of King Hugo's grown soldiers to
shame.

"Thank you," Tom wheezed. "But I
don't think we can beat Kaptiva here
in her own domain. The air itself is
poisoned. We can't fight if we can

barely breathe."

"Tom's right," Elenna said. "We need to get out of this forest, fast."

Tom broke into a loping jog, the closest thing to a run he could manage, heading once more for the forest's edge. Elenna and Miandra ran too, and together, they half-lurched, half-stumbled over the heaving ground through the lazy blizzard of sooty flakes. It was like trying to run in a nightmare – impossible! Tom tumbled to his knees, then staggered up. Elenna fell next, skinning a hand as she landed on a root. Somehow Miandra managed to stay upright, but then the earth gave a tremendous jolt, throwing all three of them into each other so they landed in a tangled heap. As they struggled to find their feet, a mighty crash rang out nearby. Tom glanced over and saw that a huge tree had toppled. With a grating creak, another tree listed. *BOOM!* It hit the ground and was followed almost instantly by another. Soon the whole forest was filled with thunderous crashes and bangs. A mighty *crack!* rang out just behind Tom, followed by a scream.

Elenna!

Tom spun around, his heart in his throat, to see her lying on the forest floor, a colossal branch pinning her legs. Right away, he could see that

one of
Elenna's
feet was
pointing
away at a
hideous
angle. He
swallowed
hard.
*Her leg's
broken!*

1

SITTING DUCKS

Adrenaline flooding his veins, Tom knelt at Elenna's side. The crooked wrongness of her lower leg made his heart clench.

"Miandra, I'm going to need your help," Tom said. "We must act fast."

"I'm ready," the girl said, her eyes wide but her jaw firmly set.

"When I lift the branch, I want

you to pull Elenna to safety." Tom turned back to his friend. Her face was as pale as ash and contorted in pain. "Elenna – I am sorry, but this is going to hurt." Elenna gritted her teeth and nodded.

Calling once more on the magic of his golden breastplate, Tom wrapped both arms around the branch, braced himself, then heaved it up.

Without a moment's delay, Miandra slipped her own arms under Elenna's and tugged her clear. The scream that tore from Elenna's throat pierced Tom to the core. He let the bough fall and he dropped to her side.

Elenna's breath was coming in short, shuddering gasps.

"I'm going to heal you with my green jewel," Tom said, unclipping the stone from its place in his belt.

"No…time…" Elenna managed

through gritted teeth. "Kaptiva…will come."

Glancing around at the trees that hemmed them in on every side, Tom realised Elenna was right. Through the power of his red jewel, he could feel the Beast's hateful energy close by. She could even be watching them now – one decaying tree hidden among many. Even with his green jewel, Elenna's wounds would take time and attention to heal. And all the while, they would be sitting ducks.

"I can help," Miandra said. Tom looked at Elenna, who now had her eyes squeezed shut. Sweat beaded her pale skin. The thought of leaving her wrenched at his heart, but he knew there was no other option. He hastily pressed his green jewel into Miandra's palm.

"Hold this against every part of her injury until it heals," Tom told her. "I'll distract Kaptiva." With one final, agonised glance at his friend, Tom grabbed his sword and shield then turned away and broke into a run.

Adrenaline was still fizzing through his body, sharpening his senses and lending him new strength. The rise and fall of the forest floor barely troubled him now. The sooty flakes that filled the air were nothing compared to Elenna's pain. He touched his hand to the red jewel in his belt as he sprinted through the gloom, putting as much distance between himself and his injured friend as he could.

I'm over here, you mouldy old log! Tom called to Kaptiva with his mind. *Follow me if you dare!*

Before long, he began to hear a creaking, slithering hiss: the sound of the tree-Beast gliding along on her snaking roots. He smiled grimly. *It's working...*

Weaving a chaotic path through the trees, Tom raced over the undulating ground. *Where are you, then?* he goaded, though he knew Kaptiva had to be close. *I can't see you... You're probably too slow and lumbering to ever catch me!*

Kaptiva roared, her voice booming like thunder as it filled Tom's mind. *I will catch you – and when I do, I will tear your body apart!*

Tom burst out from under the trees and into a clearing. *Perfect!* The open space was just what he needed. He stopped and turned slowly, listening for the tell-tale slither of Kaptiva's pursuit. The only sound that greeted him was the howl of the wind.

There's nowhere for you to hide from me here, Tom called to the Beast. *Come and feel the bite of my sword if you aren't too afraid.*

Little fool... Kaptiva replied. *I am here before you, right now, and yet you see me not!*

Tom ran his eyes around the circle of trees once more. All were as warped and crooked as the Beast. Then he spotted a tiny scrap of white – one of Elenna's feather-fletched arrows stuck in a trunk.

There you are, he thought.

Letting his eyes drift onwards, as if he had missed the sign, Tom gathered his strength together. Then, calling on the magic of his golden boots, he leapt towards the Beast, swinging his sword in a wide arc. Kaptiva's red eyes snapped open as Tom drew close. One of her lower branches struck out, swiping for him.

Arching his body in mid-flight, Tom dodged the blow and slashed his blade across the Beast's trunk, opening a deep gouge. Kaptiva

screamed in pain and fury, red eyes flaring bright and amber spewing from her jagged jaws.

Die! she howled, swinging a huge knobbly branch down towards Tom's head. Tom dived sideways, but another branch whipped out, forcing him to parry with his sword. More branches swished through the air in a frenzied attack. He took some on his shield, each one sending a shockwave down his arm, but he couldn't keep track of the blows raining down. One sneaked underneath and struck his chest, cracking a rib. As he gasped in pain, a slender white tendril of root clamped shut around his wrist, trapping his sword arm.

Kaptiva yanked, alost wrenching Tom's arm from its socket. He half-skidded, half-stumbled towards the Beast as she dragged him in close, pulling his arm above his head then forcing it right up against the gnarled bark of her trunk. With his face almost touching Kaptiva, Tom heard her let out a bubbling hiss of satisfaction as she pressed the length of his forearm into the oozing cut he had sliced a moment before. Tom tried to wrench his arm free as amber flowed from the gash, coating his sleeve, hardening fast. Finally, Kaptiva uncoiled her root from his wrist, letting it go. But Tom found he still couldn't move his arm at all. It was stuck fast in a layer of solid amber. Panic burned inside his chest. *I'm trapped!*

Suddenly, Tom heard running feet from behind him, approaching fast. Elenna's voice came from somewhere nearby. "Tom, where are you?"

Tom opened his lips to call a warning. Before he could utter a word, a mouldy branch slapped tightly over his mouth to gag him. Stowing his shield on his back, Tom tried to prise the branch away from his face with his free hand. It was no use: he just succeeded in tearing off chunks

of bark. He tugged again at his sword arm, but it was completely stuck. Then suddenly, he heard Kaptiva speak – not into his mind this time. His blood ran cold as Kaptiva called out in a voice that was a perfect imitation of Tom's own.

"I'm over here, Elenna," the Beast cried. "Everything's fine. I've defeated Kaptiva!"

Tom heard Elenna breathe an audible sigh of relief. Her footsteps quickened, hurrying towards him. He yanked frantically at his trapped arm. His fingers tore at the branch on his face, but he couldn't budge it. He tried to shout but couldn't even force a muffled cry past the rotten wood clamped over his mouth. Helpless fury burned inside him.

Elenna's walking into a trap!

7

KAPTIVA'S FINAL STAND

The more Tom struggled, the tighter Kaptiva gripped him. He tasted blood as the branch covering his mouth ground his lips into his teeth. *Elenna!* he cried out inside, wishing he could reach her through his red jewel. Wishing she could read his mind. But it was hopeless.

"You missed all the action," Kaptiva called out in Tom's voice. "Come and look, the wretched Beast is dead! I've killed her!"

Tom heard the approaching footsteps falter, as if Elenna had stopped to listen. A heartbeat later, the steps started up again. Tom struggled harder than ever, listening as his friend raced into Kaptiva's trap…

"Tom would never speak like that!" Elenna cried as she stepped into the clearing with Miandra and let an arrow fly. *Thud!* The missile struck Kaptiva somewhere far above Tom's head. He felt a judder run through the Beast's trunk, and gasped with pain as her grip on his face squeezed tighter. Tom heard Elenna fire another arrow. Kaptiva howled, her branches thrashing wildly.

I can't waste the chance Elenna has given me, Tom thought, his mind racing for a way to escape. Then he had it.

With the Beast distracted, Tom took his chance. Using his feet to push his body away from Kaptiva's trunk, he reached his free hand forwards into the gap he had made. Next, he opened his pinned hand and let his weapon fall. With perfect timing, Tom caught the hilt of his sword, left-handed. Then, glancing

 up to
find his
mark,
he drove
his blade
into the
Beast's
open eye,
sinking
the
weapon
in up to
the hilt.

Kaptiva's body convulsed in
agony. Tom lost his grip on his sword
as sticky amber flowed from the
Beast's eye towards him. Once again,
the horrible image of the trapped

Janus birds filled his mind.

While there's blood in my veins, I will not die like that! Tom could feel Kaptiva's grip on him weakening. *It's now or never!* Calling on the strength of his golden breastplate, Tom wrenched the Beast's mouldy branch away from his mouth. Then he bent both legs, bracing his feet against the shuddering wood of Kaptiva's trunk, and kicked out hard, propelling himself backwards. White-hot pain flared in his arm as the skin was torn from the solidified amber that held it, but he was free, flying through the air. He tucked into a backwards roll as he soared, then landed squarely on his feet, right between Elenna and

Miandra.

"Go, Tom!" Elenna said, clapping him on the back. Letting out a tremendous roar of anger and pain, Kaptiva lowered one of her quivering branches towards her eye and yanked Tom's blade free. Sap spurted from the wound, spilling down her face. With a flick of the branch, Kaptiva hurled Tom's sword, sending it spinning towards him. Just in time, he snatched his shield from his back and lifted it. *Thunk!* The blade ricocheted off the wood.

Before Tom could retrieve his weapon, Kaptiva opened her giant red mouth wider than ever, and sprayed a torrent of amber in all directions.

"Get behind my shield," Tom shouted to Miandra and Elenna. But instead of doing as she was asked, Miandra darted to one side and began to hop between the puddles, neatly dodging Kaptiva's deadly spray until she drew close to the crazed Beast's convulsing trunk. Letting her trident fall, Miandra lifted her jewelled net with both hands and stuffed it into the Beast's open mouth, stemming the flood of amber.

Tom collected his fallen sword and watched in amazement as liquid amber began to build up behind the net. Kaptiva's eyes rolled, and a hideous choking sound came from deep within her trunk. Bending branches towards her red mouth, Kaptiva clawed at the net, trying to tear it free, but it was stuck fast, frozen in place by the viscous resin that was quickly hardening.

"Good shot!" Tom said as Miandra sprinted back to join him and Elenna. Miandra flashed him a shy smile.

Tom brandished his sword. "Let's

finish this now!" he said – but
suddenly, a white root shot out like a
lasso, grabbed Miandra by the waist
and snatched her up into the air.

Tom stared in horror as the Beast
turned and fled into the forest,
spattering amber as she went and
taking Miandra with her.

A STICKY END

Tom and Elenna charged after Kaptiva, dodging between pools of sticky amber. Miandra was struggling helplessly above the ground, held in the Beast's grip.

As they passed Miandra's trident, Elenna snatched it up and hurled it towards the Beast's trailing roots. The three-pronged weapon sliced through pale wood and pinned a thick tendril to the ground. Kaptiva turned, her injured eye gummed almost shut, but the other eye flashing with rage.

"Give me the jewel my master craves!" Kaptiva hissed, from the corner of her mouth. Though the voice she used was muffled and distorted, it was uncannily like Malvel's. "If you do not, I shall rip this little thing to bits." Tom watched in horror as Kaptiva's branches snaked around Miandra's arms and legs, gripping tight, then started to pull. The girl's eyes widened in terror and pain, but she shook her head.

"Don't do it, Tom!" Miandra shouted.

"Tom, you have to!" Elenna countered. "We can't let Miandra die!"

With Malvel's voice still echoing in his head, Tom  remembered what Elenna had told him earlier – about never trusting the wizard. A plan began to form in his mind.

"All right!" Tom shouted at the Beast. "You win." He took the purple jewel from his belt and crossed the clearing towards Kaptiva, his head bowed in defeat.

Stopping before the Beast's trunk, right below Miandra, Tom held out the purple jewel on his palm.

"You act wisely," Kaptiva snarled in Malvel's voice. The tree-Beast lowered a spindly branch, reaching for the jewel. But before the mouldy wood could brush Tom's hand, he hurled the purple stone back behind him, towards Elenna.

Then, gripping his sword with both hands like an axe, Tom drew on all the magical strength of his golden breastplate, and every scrap of power that was left in his body, and swung his blade.

THUNK! Tom chopped a deep gouge in Kaptiva's trunk, then chopped again. *SMACK!*

A mighty quiver ran through Kaptiva's broad trunk, all the way up to her branches. With another great shudder, the Beast released her grip on Miandra, letting the girl fall. Sidestepping the resin now pouring from Kaptiva's trunk, Tom dropped his sword and extended his arms to catch Miandra before she could hit the ground. He set her down lightly then picked up his sword again. He turned back to the shuddering tree-Beast and sent one final, mighty blow thudding into the rotten wood. *CRACK!* Tom leapt back as dark brown amber surged from the new wound, pooling around the Beast's roots. Kaptiva's single good eye opened wide and round, then flickered and went dark. The torrent

of amber slowed and finally ran dry. Kaptiva rocked backwards – once, twice – then, with an ear-splitting creak, she fell.

BOOM! The sound of the huge tree hitting the ground echoed like thunder, rolling and rumbling until, finally, silence fell, and all was still. Blinking as if awakening from a dream, Tom turned to check on his friends.

Miandra had scratches all over her arms and face, but she looked otherwise unharmed. Beneath the remains of her leggings, Elenna's shins showed no sign of their horrific wounds, and she held Tom's purple jewel in her hand. Tom glanced down at his forearm. Crusted amber still coated what was left of his sleeve, and his skin was pink and weeping underneath, but he knew it would heal.

Elenna grinned. "You had me fooled for a moment there," she said. "I really thought you were going to give up the jewel. In fact, I thought you had no choice."

Tom smiled too. "Trusting Malvel to keep his word was no choice at all," he said. "You told me that, remember?"

Elenna smiled. "I did, didn't I?"

Miandra had stepped closer to Kaptiva, right to the edge of the sheeny pool of amber. She frowned at the decayed wood of the Beast's trunk.

"How can we be sure she's really dead?" Miandra asked, turning back to Tom. "After all, she has no heartbeat for us to check."

Tom gestured to the ground beneath his feet. "The forest floor stopped moving when she fell," Tom said. "And look…" He pointed to the trees at the edge of the clearing. Long thorns and sticky-looking maroon leaf buds were already sprouting on the branches of the trees, which were standing straighter than before.

"This forest may never be the perfect spot for a stroll," Tom said, "but it will live again, now that Kaptiva is gone."

Miandra tipped her head thoughtfully. "I'm glad she's gone. Kaptiva was rotten, right to the core, and she was able to make us hear anything she wanted. I know now that you were right. My mother was never here at all."

Tom nodded. "Speaking of your mother, she will be worried. It's time we sent you home. I'm sorry you can't take your fishing net with you, but you can be proud that it was lost helping to defeat a Beast."

"I can make a new net," Miandra said. She reached into a pocket and handed Tom his green jewel, which he tucked into his belt. "I am ready to go home."

Elenna gave back the purple jewel too. Figuring Miandra must be hungry, Tom brought a memory into his mind of the palace kitchens back in Tangala. As he held up the jewel, focussing on the image, the stone began to pulse with warmth. Tom sketched a large rectangle in the air, starting and ending at the ground. As soon as the shape was complete, the air shimmered, and a view of a long flour-dusted bench appeared, covered in cooling loaves of bread. Tom could hear the clatter of pans and the sound of merry chatter. His stomach twisted with hunger at the smell of freshly baked bread.

Miandra walked towards the portal, then turned back to Tom. "Even though I almost died on this Quest," she said solemnly, "I believe that while there is breath in my body, fighting Beasts will be my destiny."

"You have proved yourself courageous and resourceful," Tom said. "Tangala would be lucky to have you as its champion." Miandra

flashed Tom one of her rare, fleeting smiles, then stepped through the portal. It instantly vanished behind her, leaving the lingering scent of baking bread hanging in the air.

Elenna groaned. "What I wouldn't give for just one bite of that bread!" she said.

"I know what you mean," Tom said. "But next time we open that portal, we'll be heading through it too. There's just one more young candidate to rescue first."

As they traced their path back through the forest, Tom noticed changes all around them. Ancient-looking ferns in shades of purple and mauve were unfurling beneath the trees. Red shoots poked up from the ground, and waxy-looking flowers opened their petals, revealing pointed green teeth inside.

"I'm glad the forest is recovering," Elenna said. "But I'll also be glad if I never set foot in… Wait." She was frowning. "Did you hear something?"

Tom shook his head but then he heard a muffled voice.

They followed the sound, passing beneath the last of the trees, now covered in thorns and spiky leaves, and Tom noticed a yellowed sheet of parchment lying on the ground.

"The map," he said, picking it up and turning it over.

"You're alive!" Zarlo cried happily. "I was worried that without me to lead the way, you'd perish for sure. But now you've got me back! The wind blew me all over the place, then dropped me here. And now you've found me! How lucky is that?"

"Well, I suppose it's about time we had a bit of good luck," Elenna said. "Although it would be even better if it stretched to finding some clean water to drink."

Tom rolled up Zarlo's map and tucked it inside his tunic. "Luck has never saved us on a Quest before," he said. "We don't need luck when we've got courage, determination, and strength of heart – which we're going to need if we're to survive our next brush with Malvel."

Elenna smiled. "All that, and friendship too, of course!"

THE END

CONGRATULATIONS, YOU HAVE COMPLETED THIS QUEST!

At the end of each chapter you were awarded a special gold coin.
The QUEST in this book was worth an amazing 8 coins.

Look at the Beast Quest totem picture opposite to see how far you've come in your journey to become

MASTER OF THE BEASTS.

The more books you read, the more coins you will collect!

Do you want your own
Beast Quest Totem?

1. Cut out and collect the coin below
2. Go to the Beast Quest website
3. Download and print out your totem
4. Add your coin to the totem

www.beastquest.co.uk

READ THE BOOKS, COLLECT THE COINS!
EARN COINS FOR EVERY CHAPTER YOU READ!

550+ COINS
MASTER OF THE BEASTS

550+
515
480
445
410
395
380
365
350
320
290
260
230
217
206
191
180
146
112
78
44
30
19
8

410 COINS
HERO

350 COINS
WARRIOR

230 COINS
KNIGHT

180 COINS
SQUIRE

44 COINS
PAGE

8 COINS
APPRENTICE

READ ALL THE BOOKS IN SERIES 28:
THE NETHERWORLD!

OSSIRON
THE FLESHLESS KILLER

STYX
THE LURKING TERROR

KAPTIVA
THE SHRIEKING SIREN

VELAKRO
THE LIGHTNING BIRD

*Don't miss the next
exciting Beast Quest
book: VELAKRO
THE LIGHTNING
BIRD!*

*Read on for a sneak
peek...*

THE FINAL BEAST

"What I wouldn't give for a warm
fireplace and a bowl of soup
right now," Elenna said, her teeth
chattering against a driving wind
that was cold and sharp as steel.

Tom stamped his feet as he trudged

across the desolate black stone that stretched endlessly ahead, trying to get some feeling back into his numb toes. Kaptiva's forest lay far behind them. With night fallen, it was impossible to tell where the horizon became the sky.

"I would do anything to get out of this place, too," he said. "We only have one more candidate to rescue. Then we can leave the Netherworld for good." Tom hated to think of Rafe out here on his own. The boy from Tangala had grown up as an apprentice blacksmith, just like Tom, and Tom had felt an instant liking for the tall, muscular boy, with his mop of fair hair and shy manner.

We'll never let you win Malvel, Tom thought, gritting his teeth. We've saved Nolan, Katya and Miandra from your Evil Netherworld Beasts. And we'll save Rafe! Tangala will have its Master of the Beasts!

Tom scanned for any sign of a landmark. There was nothing. He turned to Elenna. "Are we heading the right way?"

Elenna let out a heavy sigh and drew out the parchment Daltec had given them. The map had been made long ago by an eccentric wizard called Zarlo who had become trapped inside it. Before she unfurled the scroll, she raised an eyebrow towards Tom. "I still think it's odd that the map found its way back to us."

Tom nodded, unease stirring in his gut. Zarlo's map had been snatched from his hand by an enchanted wind just before their battle with Kaptiva. In a stroke of luck that seemed almost too good to be true, he and Elenna had found the map on the ground after defeating the tree Beast.

Before Tom could reply, a voice boomed from the parchment.

"Hello, friends! How wonderful that we are all together again."

"Don't you mean, why aren't we dead yet?" Elenna asked dryly. "That's normally your first question."

Zarlo chuckled. "I may have had my doubts that you'd survive the Netherworld initially, but you have proved my fears unfounded. Three Beasts defeated already! Extraordinary. I don't think you'll find the next one much of a challenge."

"What do you know of it?" Tom asked.

"Oh, she's barely a Beast at all," Zarlo said. "More an oversized bird really. Her name is Velakro, and she's only a little bigger than an eagle. Defeating her should be a doddle!"

Leaning over the map, Tom spotted the small smudge of purple light that showed where the Beast was. It glowed close to a jagged coastline, still a long way off.

"We'd better get moving," he said pacing onwards.

"What did you make of all that 'not much of a challenge stuff'?" Elenna asked once she'd tucked Zarlo's scroll away.

"Well, I've never heard a Beast described as a doddle before," Tom said. "But at least Zarlo's sounding more cheerful."

"Hmmm," Elenna said. "That's what I mean. He's not his usual grouchy self."

Tom nodded. "There's nothing we can do but keep going. Zarlo's our only hope of finding Rafe. But you're right. We should be on our guard."

Slowly, the sky lightened to the heavy brooding purple of the Netherworld day. The barren rock beneath their feet began to slope upwards, gently at first, before getting rapidly steeper. Tom and Elenna were soon bent double with the effort of climbing into the wind. Gasping, his leg muscles burning, Tom focussed his mind on Rafe. While there's blood in my veins I won't give up until we find you!

Elenna suddenly stopped. "What is that noise?" At first Tom could only hear the howling of the wind, but then he made out another, deeper sound. A low, rhythmic whooshing accompanied by a hollow boom. He remembered the craggy coastline from Zarlo's map.

"We're near the sea," Tom said, a rush of adrenaline giving him new strength. "The next Beast isn't far." He loosened his sword in its scabbard and Elenna drew her bow from her back.

The slope levelled suddenly, and the rocky ground came to a jagged halt: a cliff. Tom and Elenna stepped to the edge and peered downwards.

Elenna gasped and recoiled from the plunging drop. Tom felt suddenly dizzy. Rugged shelves of glassy black rock fell away below them, each splattered with layers of green sludge. Even more alarming were the birds perched wing to wing on every ledge, their dark blue and red bodies pressed close together. As Tom looked at their tiered ranks, they all turned at once to look up at him as if controlled by a single mind. Hundreds - no thousands! - of glinting black eyes stared at Tom, filled with cold, alien hatred.

Read
VELAKRO THE LIGHTNING BIRD
to find out what happens next!